Grubble Trouble

Hilda Offen

Collins

For Rebecca Spence and Tim Hill

Look out for more *Jets* **from Collins**
Jessy Runs Away • *Best Friends* • **Rachel Anderson**
Ivana the Inventor • *Ernest the Heroic Lion Tamer* • **Damon Burnard**
Two Hoots • *Almost Goodbye Guzzler* • **Helen Cresswell**
Shadows on the Barn • **Sarah Garland**
Nora Bone • *The Mystery of Lydia Dustbin's Diamonds* • **Brough Girling**
Thing on Two Legs • *Thing in a Box* • **Diana Hendry**
Desperate for a Dog • *More Dog Trouble* • **Rose Impey**
Georgie and the Dragon • *Georgie and the Planet Raider* • **Julia Jarman**
Cowardy Cowardy Cutlass • *Free With Every Pack* • **Robin Kingsland**
Mossop's Last Chance • *Mum's the Word* • **Michael Morpurgo**
Hiccup Harry • *Harry Moves House* • **Chris Powling**
Rattle and Hum, Robot Detectives • **Frank Rodgers**
Our Toilet's Haunted • **John Talbot**
Rhyming Russell • *Messages* • **Pat Thomson**
Monty the Dog Who Wears Glasses • *Monty's Ups and Downs* • **Colin West**
Ging Gang Goolie, it's an Alien • *Stone the Crows, it's a Vacuum Cleaner* •
Bob Wilson

First published by A & C Black Ltd in 1993
Published by Collins in 1994
10 9 8 7 6 5
Collins is an imprint of HarperCollins*Publishers*Ltd,
77–85 Fulham Palace Road, Hammersmith, London W6 8JB

ISBN 0 00 674880 5

Text and illustrations © Hilda Offen 1993

The author and the illustrator assert the moral right to
be identified as the author and the illustrator of the work.
A CIP record for this title is available from the British Library.
Printed and bound in Great Britain by
Caledonian International Book Manufacturing Ltd, Glasgow

Chapter 1

This is Nigel Goodchild. He lives at Number Thirteen, Milton Street.

You might think thirteen's an unlucky number – Nigel did.

Because next door, at Number Fifteen lived

the **Grubble family**

All I want is some peace and quiet!

Yah! Boo!

Boo!

Nigel Goodchild is a wimp!

Grandma Grubble

Mrs Grubble

Snapper

Grr!

Mr Grubble

Kevin

Kelly

3

The Grubbles were the most
unpopular family in town.

They especially liked picking on Nigel.

He wasn't safe anywhere.

'That does it! I can't stand this any longer,' said Nigel as a ball came crashing through the window and hit his model dinosaur.

He made himself some jam
sandwiches and packed them into
his rucksack.

Then he took his telescope and his
tent and set off for Grindley Wood.

But as he crept down the street he walked straight into Grandma Grubble.

BUMP

'Look where you're going, wimp!' she yelled and she *sprayed* his trainers bright pink.

Nigel ran for it.

He didn't stop running until he reached the wood. He found a peaceful clearing and pitched his tent. Then he took out his telescope.

Now for some bird-watching

A sudden movement caught his eye. Something furry was swinging through the trees.

Seconds later it dropped to the ground and raced away.

But Nigel had no time to think about what he'd seen. There was a wild yell . . . and Kevin, Kelly and Snapper jumped out of the bushes!

Within seconds, Nigel's tent was in a heap on the ground and his telescope had disappeared into the pond.

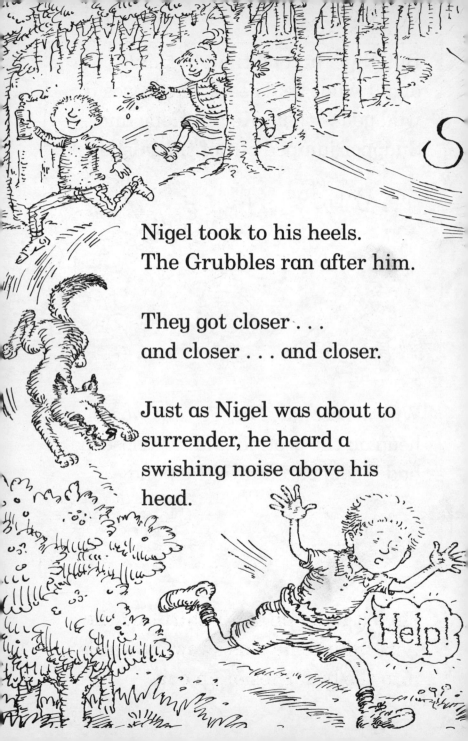

Nigel took to his heels.
The Grubbles ran after him.

They got closer . . .
and closer . . . and closer.

Just as Nigel was about to
surrender, he heard a
swishing noise above his
head.

Help!

He felt a tug on his T-shirt and the
next minute he was swept upwards
into the branches of an oak.

Chapter 2

Dazed, but in one piece, Nigel
looked up. Before him stood the
furry figure he had spotted earlier.
And it wasn't looking very happy.

You hooligan!
How dare you
disturb the
peace of my
woods?

I'm not a
hooligan! I'm
Nigel Goodchild

'They're the hooligans,'
stammered Nigel, pointing at
the Grubbles. 'I came here
for a bit of peace and quiet.'

Woof!

He went
this way!

'Hmm!' said the furry figure.

'Who are you, anyway?'
asked Nigel. 'And why are
you wearing fancy dress?'

'I'm Rabbit Girl!' said the
creature. 'The Guardian of
Grindley Wood. And this
isn't fancy dress – it's a
very warm and practical suit.'

'How long have you lived here?'
asked Nigel.

'Since I was a baby,'
said Rabbit Girl. 'I was
lost in the wood and
brought up by a family
of rabbits.'

'Rabbits?' repeated Nigel.

'Yes, stupid! You know, furry animals
with long ears and twitchy
noses!' said Rabbit Girl.

And she began to tell Nigel about
her life in the wild.

I eat nuts and berries... I drink from streams... I understand animal language... I have a special whistle... climb like a squirrel... I can run like a rabbit... I live in a burrow...

Eek! Eek! Eek!

15

'Please!' begged Nigel.

'And can you whistle?' asked
Rabbit Girl.

'Whistling is the most important
thing of all,' said Rabbit Girl.
'No whistle – no job!'

And with that, she grabbed Nigel round the waist, leapt on to a springy branch, and swung him down to the ground.

They walked back to Nigel's camp and Rabbit Girl rescued Nigel's telescope.

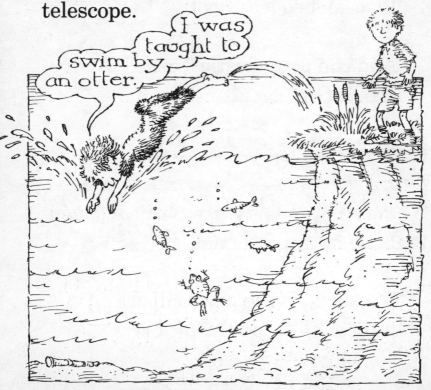

As Nigel packed up his tent, Rabbit Girl's nose began to twitch.

Rabbit Girl started to shovel down the sandwiches as fast as she could.

'Perhaps,' she said, with her mouth full, 'perhaps – if you brought me jam sandwiches every Saturday, you *could* be my assistant.'

Chapter 3

Nigel went home and started to practise. His whistling didn't get any better, but he did begin to pick up a bit of animal talk.

He took up weight-training before breakfast and exercised regularly.

He even stayed on after school
for athletics.

Every Saturday, Nigel made a big pile of jam sandwiches and cycled into Grindley Wood.

Rabbit Girl always seemed pleased to see him. 'I'm much better at running and jumping and climbing,' said Nigel each week.

Rabbit Girl didn't
seem very impressed.
'I don't think I'll ever
make it,' thought Nigel
gloomily. But then
something happened
that changed everything.

Chapter 4

It was early one Saturday morning. Nigel was in the backyard, practising his whistle, when he heard the Grubbles discussing their plans for the day.

'Oh no!' thought Nigel. 'They'll wreck the wood!' He jumped on his bike and pedalled off as fast as he could.

'Rabbit Girl,' cried Nigel, 'Rabbit Girl!'

Rabbit Girl stuck her head out of a burrow.

Where are my sandwiches?

Never mind that now – the Grubbles are coming!

But even as Nigel spoke, the Grubble's pick-up truck rattled into the wood.

PEEP! PEEP!

'Everybody out!' cried Mr Grubble.
He grabbed his axe. 'We'll have a
bonfire!'

'We'll cook a duck on it!' said
Grandma Grubble.

And they all disappeared amongst
the trees.

'Come on, Nigel,
we've got work to
do,' said Rabbit Girl.

Mr Grubble stopped before an ancient oak. He raised his axe . . . and blinked in amazement. There before him stood Nigel Goodchild.

All of a sudden,
there was a swishing
sound in the trees
above and the axe was
snatched from his
hands. Mr Grubble
caught a glimpse
of something furry
whizzing through
the air. Then it
was gone.

snatch

What's
going
on?

Not far away, Grandma Grubble
was stalking a duck.

She did not hear Rabbit Girl's high-
pitched whistle . . . nor did she
notice Snapper leave her side and
bound into the bushes.

Good boy!

Rabbit Girl whispered something in Snapper's ear. The next moment Snapper leapt from the bushes straight at Grandma Grubble, who was just taking aim.

Grandma Grubble lost her balance and toppled forward. She hit the water with a mighty splash.

'Hurry!' called Rabbit
Girl. 'We're needed
over here.'

Kevin Grubble was
halfway up a pine tree.
There was a nest full
of eggs at the top.
Rabbit Girl whistled
and the air filled
with birds.

They flew at Kevin
Grubble and started
to mob him.

'Help!' cried Kevin as
he lost his grip, and
'Ow!' he squealed as
he landed upside down
in a holly bush.

But Rabbit Girl and Nigel were already off. They had heard Mrs Grubble singing, and they knew she was up to no good.

Then Nigel had a really good idea.

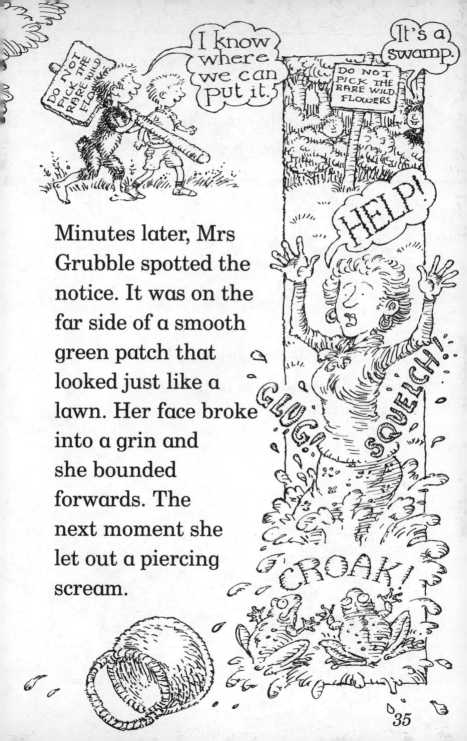

I know where we can put it.

It's a swamp.

DO NOT PICK THE RARE WILD FLOWERS

DO NOT PICK THE RARE WILD FLOWERS

HELP!

GLUG!

SQUELCH!

CROAK!

Minutes later, Mrs Grubble spotted the notice. It was on the far side of a smooth green patch that looked just like a lawn. Her face broke into a grin and she bounded forwards. The next moment she let out a piercing scream.

Chapter 5

The Grubbles staggered back to their picnic site. They were in a terrible state.

'Never mind,' said Mrs Grubble,
'let's have a game of football.
I need to dry off.'

Rabbit Girl's nose began to twitch.

It's coming from the hamper!

Mmm!

'Don't go!' said Nigel. 'Someone will see you.'

But Rabbit Girl was already wriggling off through the long grass. She reached the hamper and stretched out a hand.

At that moment the ball came bouncing towards her, with Mr Grubble chasing after it.

He spotted Rabbit Girl at once. He
sneaked up behind her and – just as
she was about to take her first bite –
he tipped her into the hamper!

Then he sat on the lid.

Nigel watched as the Grubbles
gathered round.

Mr Grubble took a strong rope and wound it round the hamper. Then he tied a knot in it.

'I must get help,' thought Nigel and he turned and ran off into the wood.

Now was his chance to prove himself.
He took a deep breath and blew.
Nothing happened. He had another go.

Still there wasn't a sound.

'I'll never get the hang of this,' he
moaned.
He gave it one last try . . . and out
came one long, perfect whistle.

Then he did it again.

All at once the wood was filled with the sound of scampering feet and fluttering wings. There were foxes and badgers and deer; there were sparrows and crows; there were cats from the town. Even Snapper came running.

Using his best animal talk, Nigel
told Snapper to dig a hole.

More animals joined in and the hole
got deeper and deeper.

Then Nigel had a
word with the birds,
and they flew off to
collect all sorts
of greenery.

When the hole was deep enough,
they covered it with branches,
leaves and twigs.

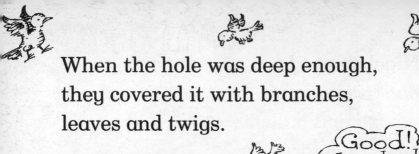

Then Nigel ran back to the picnic
site.

The Grubbles were
arguing over
what to do with
Rabbit Girl.

Nigel stepped out from behind a bush and pulled a horrible face.

The Grubbles could hardly believe their eyes.

'Grab him!' yelled
Mr Grubble as Nigel
jumped a stream.

'Come on down!'
Mrs Grubble cried as
he shot up a tree.

'Just wait till we get our hands
on you!' they screamed
as they watched him
swinging overhead.

'Come back here!' they roared as he ran nimbly across a fallen log.

And all the time Nigel was leading them deeper and deeper into the wood.

Almost there!

'We've got him!' roared Mr Grubble.

Nigel reached the pit. He gave a
bound and soared right over. The
Grubbles just kept running . . .

'Aargh!' they cried as they felt the ground give way beneath them.

'Help!' they screamed as they plunged into the darkness below.

Chapter 6

Nigel peered into the pit.

The Grubbles jumped up and down and shook their fists and shouted some terrible things.

Nigel signalled to
the animals to come
out of their hiding
places. 'Guard them!'
he ordered. 'And make
sure they don't escape.'

Then Nigel raced back to the
Grubbles' picnic site.

He untied the rope and Rabbit Girl
leapt out of the hamper. Her face
was covered in jam.

Nigel grabbed the rope and led
the way back to the pit.

The Grubbles had quietened down
and were beginning to look rather
sorry for themselves.

'If we let you out, you must promise to change,' said Rabbit Girl.

For once the Grubbles didn't argue.

'Cross your hearts
and hope to die?'
said Nigel.

'Yes! Yes! Just get
us out of here!'
they cried.

Nigel threw the
rope down into
the pit and the
Grubbles climbed
out one by one.

'My animals will be watching you,' said Rabbit Girl. 'If you ever cause trouble again, there'll be worse in store for you.'

The Grubbles slunk past her.

'By the way — they were the best jam sandwiches I've had since I was lost in the wood,' said Rabbit Girl.

At once the Grubbles started hugging
Rabbit Girl and smothering her
with kisses.

They explained that she was their
very own, dear little Tracy Grubble,
the baby they had lost on a picnic
all those years ago.

Rabbit Girl was not so happy.

'Please come home with us, Tracy!'
begged the Grubbles.
'I like it here,' said Rabbit Girl. 'And
please don't call me Tracy.'

'Of course he can!' cried the
Grubbles and they started
kissing Rabbit Girl
again.

Chapter 7

And that's almost the end of the
story. The Grubbles were changed
people.

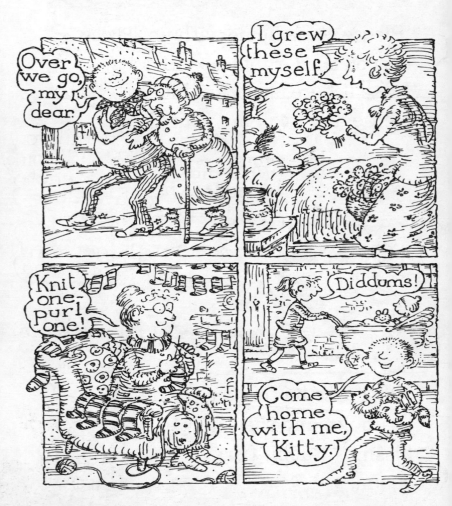

They were especially nice to Nigel –
they couldn't do enough for him.

Every Saturday Rabbit Girl left the
wood and became Tracy Grubble
for the day. The Grubbles made a
pile of jam sandwiches and went out
of their way to be pleasant.
Rabbit Girl even grew quite fond
of them all.

After tea, Nigel went back to the
wood with Rabbit Girl.

'Assistant my foot,' said Rabbit
Girl. 'Nigel Goodchild – you're my
best friend!'